I'm Trying to Tell You

BERNARD ASHLEY

Illustrated by Lyn Jones

Puffin Books

PUFFIN BOOKS

Published by the Penguin Group
Penguin Books Ltd, 27 Wrights Lane, London W8 5TZ, England
Penguin Books USA Inc., 375 Hudson Street, New York, New York 10014, USA
Penguin Books Australia Ltd, Ringwood, Victoria, Australia
Penguin Books Canada Ltd, 10 Alcorn Avenue, Toronto, Ontario, Canada M4V 3B2
Penguin Books (NZ) Ltd, 182–190 Wairau Road, Auckland 10, New Zealand

Penguin Books Ltd, Registered Offices: Harmondsworth, Middlesex, England

First published by Kestrel Books 1981
Published in Puffin Books 1982
9 10

Copyright © Bernard Ashley, 1981
Illustrations copyright © Lyn Jones, 1981
All rights reserved

Printed in England by Clays Ltd, St Ives plc
Filmset in Monophoto Bembo

Contents

I should like to thank May Collins
for her help with 'Dear Bren'.

B.A.

The children from Saffin Street School, like all of us, have their stories to tell. Here are four of them, told by Nerissa Jones, Ray Smith, Lyn Ruskin, and Prakash Patel.

Nerissa Jones

Monday Morning

'Nerissa Jones, what *are* you thinking about? You're certainly not thinking about writing a story for me.'

Miss Banks sat frowning away down that room like she'd left her contacts out. Sour as a green apple, she was.

'Raymond Smith's done a page already. What have you done?'

There weren't no point in tellin' no lies. My bit of paper was as blank as that wall, and I didn't have no more idea of some 'Exciting Adventure' than that desk lid.

'I'm thinking 'bout my sister, Miss,' I said.

'Well, there's a time and a place for everything,' she comes back. 'Now get your mind on your work, girl.'

So I tried – but it's really hard, concentrating on story writing when your mind's all buzzing with other things. It's like a glass door, inside your brain, I reckon. You can shut it hard as you like, but them other thoughts still keep showing through.

I could still see all their faces, and all the fussing and the clapping, and the smart, best turn-outs. I could see my sister in her bride-frock, looking like the queen of all the world. And my daddy's smiling mouth – and his crying eyes.

And looking down, like I did a million times Saturday, I could still see my pink silk shoes, shining when I danced.

And now I was sitting at my desk, looking this time at those legs I'd had before, and the little white socks and the old brown bumpers.

You don't stay special for long, do you? It don't seem five minutes before you're back to your old self again, doing sums and having to think up Exciting Adventures.

My Auntie Lizzie got there first, long before she was wanted in the house. My mammy shouted down the stairs, ' You go sit apiece in the best room, look through them cards and presents.' But only Auntie Lizzie's Uncle Ben does what my mammy says. Auntie Lizzie's in the kitchen making tea and organizing things before you know it.

But my daddy, he's good with her. Before she makes herself a nuisance he gets her laughing, tells her an old family joke he knows she likes; and then he makes her feel important – which is only what she wants, I s'pose, being the oldest auntie of the bride. He sits her down and gets her checking the bills for the drink and the food, and the extra for the choir and bells.

That's private family business, and she feels really good.

There's been talking for weeks about how my sister has her hair. 'No fussing,' my mammy says, 'just neat with a pretty ribbon there.'

'You are joking, ain't you?' my sister says. And she threatens something *drastic* if she hears any more of that talk.

She has what she wants in the end: beautiful blown-out curls, looking like a flower in the moonlight.

When I see her coming down the stairs, I can't tell you how I feel. I want to smile till my face splits, and cry a bucket of tears, and there's this new feeling of no floor beneath my feet. And I can't breathe, too. I just stand there with my mouth open, making some funny noise or other.

And I think, 'Is this what happens, then? That girl in the next-door bed to mine – she leaves it in a heap every morning and grumbles in her sleep, and she never can find her shoes – does she come out like this, one day? Like a beautiful butterfly out of a tangly bush?'

And then riding in that big car to the church, that's something special, with those pink ribbons fluttering like they're waving hello to people. You keep your eyes on your shoes, but you're really thinking, 'It's me in here; and why can't my mates all be out in the street this Saturday morning?'

My mammy's with me; not crying. She's been keeping too busy to think about what's really happening, I reckon. But I take a sideways look, and I wonder if she might be having a think back to *her* wedding day. Different to this, by the picture. Outside a little church in Kingston back home, where the sunny white wall made the whole world look brilliant and bright.

I s'pose she must've been thinking along the same lines, because she suddenly says, 'Well, at least that old

sun's putting on a show.' And I reckon he was. He made Clapham brighten up and smile. And my mammy sits back in her seat instead of perching nervous on the front; and she closes her eyes and mumbles something quiet.

So it's all going well according to the plans. I'm the happiest person in the world except my sister; Auntie Lizzie's gone in the first car; our car's running to time; and there's just my daddy and the beautiful bride waiting for the first driver to double back and get them. Everything's perfect.

Except we turn round the corner up to the church and there isn't a living soul there.

'There ain't no wedding here today,' the driver says, sliding back his glass. 'This place is all shut up, missus, like the Lord's gone on holiday.'

'That can't be the case,' my mammy says. 'Perhaps they've all gone in and shut the doors.'

'Hey, you sure this is the right day?' the driver asks. 'Give me a look of your invitation.'

'I ain't got no invitation!' my mammy snaps. 'I'm the mother of the bride. I don't get issued with no invitation. And what d'you think I am, stupid, not knowing the right day of my own daughter's wedding? And where's that first car gone?'

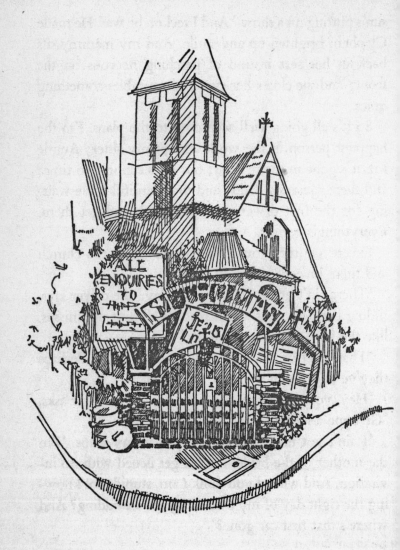

The driver shrugs his shoulders. 'Search me. But there ain't no wedding here, that's for sure. I've never seen a place look so closed up and empty.'

I was getting real edgy with this driver now. He had the look on him that, all right, we were sitting in his car, and he did have to care a bit about our problem, but he wasn't going to move no mountains for us.

'What's the name of this church you've brought us to?' I ask him, trying to put the baby back in his lap. He gives me this long stare. It's a good job for him my daddy ain't in this car, I'm thinking. He wouldn't be sitting there all don't-care if he was.

'Saint Thomas's,' he says, resting his hands on the steering-wheel. 'That's the address your fellow gave us.'

I come to, then. 'Well, I can tell you this ain't Saint Thomas's,' I tell him. 'I go to Sunday School at Saint Thomas's, and there's no way this is that place.'

The driver said nothing, but he started pointing at the notice board, all slow and cocky.

THE CHURCH OF SAINT THOMAS, CLAPHAM COMMON, it said.

'Well, what are you doing, then?' I asked him, giving my mammy and me both a surprise. 'Saint Thomas, Clapham *Junction* is what we want.'

He didn't say no more. Just muttered a bit. But didn't he drive fast, now he knew it was his mistake! One pink

ribbon came off, and the other was flapping and flying like a streamer. People had to jump out of the way just

to save their skins. My mammy closed her eyes and knocked her hat on the tilt.

You should have heard the cheers when we got our-selves there.

The bride was waiting already and my daddy was walking in all directions at once. But did their faces start to smile!

Uncle Ben stopped it being a nasty turn-out with the car people.

'You gone the long way round buying peppers?' he says to my mammy. 'You don't need to make such a big fuss of me.'

And then it all went forward like the stories tell. I carried the bride's train and never tripped, and stepped up and back when the moments came. And everyone was happy. We sang, our families, like old Saint Thomas Clapham Junction ain't never heard before. And back at home we sang and danced so hard, I never noticed I slept on my own in that bedroom till the next afternoon around two.

Now I can't get it out of my head, no matter what tricks I try. School Monday morning is all mixed up. I get the words of 'Once upon a time' down on that paper, but nothing else; and then Miss Banks is there, going on again.

'This just isn't good enough,' she says. 'Really, Nerissa Jones – haven't you got *any* ideas for an exciting story?'

Ray Smith
Sir's New Car

Sir's got a new car. You know, Mr Cox, the deputy head. It's a smart little car, all red, with black inside. He came in it the other day, and got out of it like a film star, all posh and slow.

'It can go a hundred miles an hour,' he told Miss Banks.

'Not up the High Street, I hope,' she said.

But she was only being rotten, because her car's old.

'He's ever so proud of it,' said Tom. 'It's like a new baby.'

You could see he'd washed it and made it shine. There wasn't a bit of dust on it. You could see the sun in the polish. That's saying something round our way.

A whole crowd of kids went up to it at playtime. It wasn't in Sir's old place in the corner. It was stuck right out in front for everyone to see.

We looked through the windows. It only had two seats.

'It's a sports car,' said Tom. 'My dad wants one of them.'

It was like a little palace inside, all white fur on the dashboard and things hanging down. And there weren't any splits in the seats – and no sweet-papers on the floor.

'Here, look at this, all of you!' Sandra Brown started shouting. She's always bossing about over something, but this time it sounded real. 'Look at this! Sir's been on the telly!'

'On the telly? Come off it!' I said. 'He'd have told us, wouldn't he?' I know he fancies himself a bit with his guitar, but his head goes all shaky when he sings in the hall.

All the same, Sandra Brown made us look at what she'd found. It was some badge on the front window.

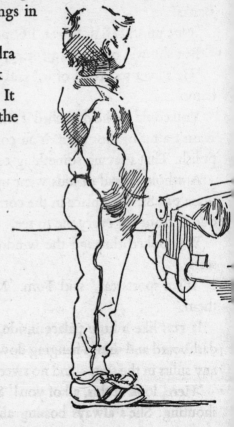

'What does that sign say, then?' she asked. 'Can't you read?'

It said TV CENTRE. CAR PARK PASS. It made your inside turn over a bit. We all looked at each other and made faces.

But I was sure Sir hadn't been on television. You don't get to miss things like that, do you? Then it came to me.

'I know,' I said. 'It's not him; but he got his car off someone else – someone who *has* been on the telly. And he's left the sticker on to show off.'

'Yeah, that's more like it,' Prakash said. And we started patting the car all over, to say we'd patted a television star's car.

When Sir came out to get us in, we asked him.

'Here, Sir, is that your car?'

'Yes,' he said, still proud, polishing off the pats with his hankie.

'Have you been on the telly?'

'I might have,' he said, with a day-dreaming look in his eyes. Then he laughed. 'I'm always up behind the North End goal at the football.'

Nerissa was looking at the number plate.

'Hey, look at this!' she shouted. She got all excited and banged her head on the mirror.

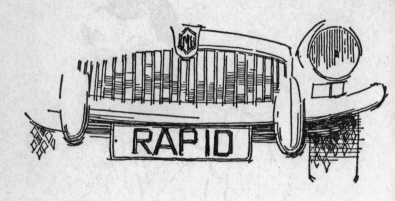

We ran round and looked at the number plate, too. RAP 1D, it said.

'So what?' I asked. 'What about it?'

Sir was still smiling. So was Nerissa.

'Can't you see?' she said. 'All you have to do is read the "One" as letter "I" – like you would if it was driving past a bit quick. What does it say then?'

'"Rapid",' I said. 'What about...Hold on! *RAPID!* Top of the charts with every record they make! It used to belong to *Rapid!*'

It made your throat go all tight.

'Did it, Sir, did it?' everyone asked.

34

Sir didn't answer, but we wanted to pat it again. Well, think of telling everyone your deputy head's got a car which used to belong to Rapid!

But Tom shut everyone up. 'Come off it!' he said. 'It's too small, isn't it? There's five in Rapid. This is only a two-seater.'

We all looked at Tom, and then at the car. It was true, what he'd said. You'd never get them all in there.

We all went a bit gloomy at that. But all of a sudden Nerissa's face cheered up – she looked like someone who's lost her dinner money but found a fiver.

'Well, it could have been *one* of them's,' she said.

'Yeah!' We started jumping about like mad things. 'That's what it is! Great!'

We looked at Sir, but he'd got one of his quiet looks on.

Prakash was still jumping. 'It's *Red*, isn't it, Sir? The one with the red guitar. It must be Red – he'd have a shining red car like this!'

Tom perked up, then. 'It's never Red's,' he said. 'This car says *Angel* to me.' You could see him spelling out Rapid in his head. After 'R' it had to be 'A'. 'Look at all that white fur, and the dangly bits like long earrings. It's a girl's car, this. Definitely.'

Sir gave him one of his mean looks.

Then everyone came in with how it had to be one or other of Rapid's cars: Red's or Angel's or Pierre's or Ida's or Donovan's. Some of the reasons were really stupid.

We all looked at him for an answer, but he didn't say anything. Not then, and not later on. He just went a bit quiet, which is unusual for him, and next time we looked he'd peeled the sticker off the window.

So we're still not sure. But somehow we lost interest in it after that. If we couldn't be sure it was Rapid who sold Sir the car, we didn't want to know.

And when you look closely, there is a bit of rust along the bottom of Sir's door. Rapid wouldn't have a rusty car, would they?

We don't talk about it any more. But sometimes when I see Sir's new car I think about it. And I reckon it was a shame, all that Rapid stuff. I think it spoilt his big day, in a funny sort of way . . .

Lyn Ruskin

Dear Bren
(a letter home from School Journey)

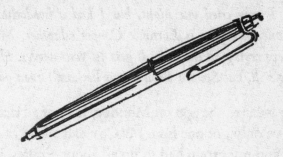

Dear Bren,

Don't drop dead because I'm writing to you. In Quiet Time we've got to write our letters to our mums and dads. It's boring – worse than being at Gran's when she's having her sleep – so at the same time as writing to them I'm writing a secret letter to you.

Sunday, 25th May

Dear Mum and Dad,

I arrived safely on School Journey. I'm glad I came. The beds are hard and the food's horrible. I'm having a great time.

In this letter I'll tell you some of the things we've been doing.

The other envelope is for Brenda. It's private!

What you said about this place was right. It's a good laugh. I only cried one night, but I had a headache. The worst one for crying is Lorraine Cooper's brother, Marvin. He keeps crying all the time. It gets on your nerves. He says his dog's ill, but Sandra Brown says he hasn't even got one.

We went to the zoo on Monday. It's not all that big. They've only got one lion. Mr Cox had a load of work cards, and my group had to do all about giraffes. It was all right, except the giraffe didn't want to come out of his shed.

Dragging round and round the zoo really makes your feet ache. Like you said, this one's dead crummy, and we all got fed up. Then Jason Ring told us to go and see what the monkeys were doing. It was great, watching them – till Miss Blake found us. She made our group go back to the giraffe. How boring!
But we kept on laughing about the monkeys . . .

In the dinner-hall we get all the meal on one tray, like in those prison films. You'll be pleased to know I'm eating all my food up. We get cooked breakfasts and the dinners here are just like at school – except there the mash is lumpy and the custard's runny, and down here they go in for lumpy custard and runny mash.

PLEASE
DO NOT
FEED

Don't you get starving down here, Bren? They don't give you half enough. Still, in Free Time, if you squeeze through the hedge at the back of the playing-field, you can run down the village shop for crisps. Did you used to do that? Half the camp's in there some nights. One of the kids said there's only one reason why we don't get caught. The teachers are all down the pub buying pies!

On Tuesday we went to look at a big white horse drawn on a hill. You can see it for miles. From the coach it looked like a big painting, but up close it's the chalk, still showing through after hundreds of years. It's really something, I reckon, lasting all that time.

You're supposed to keep off of that big white horse. There's notices there. But Tony Smith went on it and dug up a bit of chalk with his heel. He wanted it to take home for his mum, but he got scared and dropped it out the coach window. It went under this lorry's wheel and got squashed to nothing on the road.

There's eight girls in our dormitory. We get points for keeping it tidy. You get three for making your bed properly, and one for leaving the sink clean. But you lose points if you leave sweet-papers and clothes on the floor. Up to today I'm number five.

We're not all that bothered about Miss Blake's points. Stella Camp worked out our own system. You get one point for going out on the landing in your nightie, two for knocking on the boys' door and running away, and five for going down the stairs or doing something else daring. Stella's winning, but I'm second – and I've got a couple of good ideas for next week.

On Wednesday we went horse riding. We had to wear the proper hats. I went round the field twice on mine, and he galloped quite fast. The lady said I was very good.

If we cleared our shed out, we'd have room for a little pony, wouldn't we? I could go out every day and collect grass off the verge for him to eat, and wouldn't I save a lot on bus fares?

Sandra Brown said she knew all about horse riding. She reckons she goes every week. She really fancies herself, and she sat on her horse like those girls do in the pony books, with a face like some statue. But then her horse wouldn't go! He kept eating the grass, and she had to pretend she was letting him.

Our school played some games against one of the other schools on Thursday. The boys played football and the girls played netball. I was in the netball team.

We won 14–6, but the boys lost 10–0. If the teachers still want to, our school's going to play them at rounders next week.

In the football game this other school kept calling our boys a load of rubbish. And when Prakash Patel got the ball they made jungle noises. Even the teachers had a row about it. The other school won the match, but we won the fights after the teachers went in.

On Friday we saw loads of animals at the market. Mr Cox said he thought he'd bought a cow when he blew his nose in the Auction Ring. We saw all the sheep up close, and a pig as big as our bath. But I felt really sad, seeing all the animals going off to be killed.

At the market one man was really cruel to this calf. He kept prodding it hard with a sharp stick, and when he pushed it in the back of a van he made it knock its head. Anyway, when the man was having a drink, Raymond Smith gave him a sandwich. It was one the cows had licked. And the man ate it up! We felt better then. But I'm definitely going to be a vegetarian when I'm not so hungry.

Do you remember that film, *Valley of Time*? Well, we had it down here on Friday night, in the dinner-hall. It would have been good, but there were some little kids here from one of the other schools, and the teacher put his hand over the picture every time the prehistoric monster came on. We said it wasn't fair. If they weren't old enough to watch it, they should have been in bed.

In films these little cissy kids stopped us seeing the monsters. So after lights-out Tommy Dove and Raymond Smith got dressed up in sheets and crawled into their bedroom – just to make up for what they missed!

I've never heard screaming like it – anyhow, not since that spider walked across your pillow.

Yesterday we went to the seaside.
We did a project on the harbour.
We had to draw the fishermen's
sheds. We saw one of
the boats come in and
unload the catch. We
made a list of all the
different things they
caught.

Then we had fish and chips in a café. At the end, we had an hour of Free Time while we waited for the coach.

The harbour's good, isn't it, Bren? Especially the Amusements over the road. Stella and I were sick on the coach back and Miss Blake blamed the fish supper. But we'd had six goes on the Octopus. We found out if you scream a lot they let you stay on for nothing!

Well, that's nearly all I've got time for. Miss Blake says I've got to keep up the same behaviour next week.

Oh! She's just coming round to check our spellings and handwriting, and collect up all the spare bits of paper.

Sorry about screwing this page up. I made a mistake, thought it was some other bit of paper. Tell Bren I'm sorry there isn't a letter for her after all. But say it's been great on School Journey. I've really learned a lot down here.

See you on Saturday.
Your loving daughter,
Lyn

Prakash Patel
Lenny's Red-Letter Day

Lenny Fraser is a boy in my class. Well, he's a boy in my class when he comes. But to tell the truth, he doesn't come very often. He stays away from school for a week at a time, and I'll tell you where he is. He's at the shops, stealing things sometimes, but mainly just opening the doors for people. He does it to keep himself warm. I've seen him in our shop. When he opens the door for someone, he stands around inside till he gets sent out. Of course, it's quite warm enough in school, but he hates coming. He's always got long, tangled hair, not very clean, and his clothes are too big or too small, and they call him 'Flea-bag'. He sits at a desk without a partner, and no one wants to hold his hand in games. All right, they're not to blame; but he isn't, either. His mother never gets up in the morning, and his house is dirty. It's a house that everybody runs past very quickly.

But Lenny makes me laugh a lot. In the playground he's always saying funny things out of the corner of his mouth. He doesn't smile when he does it. He says these funny things as if he's complaining. For example, when Mr Cox the deputy head came to school in his new car, Lenny came too, that day; but he didn't join in all the admiration. He looked at the little car and said to me, 'Anyone missing a skateboard?'

He misses all the really good things, though – the School Journeys and the outing. And it was a big shame about his birthday.

It happens like this with birthdays in our class. Miss Blake lets everyone bring their cards and perhaps a small present to show the others. Then everyone sings 'Happy Birthday' and we give them bumps in the playground. If people can't bring a present, they tell everyone what they've got instead. I happen to know some people make up the things that they've got just to be up with the others, but Miss Blake says it's good to share our Red-Letter Days.

I didn't know about these Red-Letter Days before. I thought they were something special in the post, like my dad handles in his Post Office in the shop. But Miss Blake told us they are red printed words in the prayer books, meaning special days.

Well, what I'm telling you is that Lenny came to school on his birthday this year. Of course, he didn't tell us it was his birthday, and, as it all worked out, it would have been better if Miss Blake hadn't noticed it in the register. But, 'How nice!' she said. 'Lenny's here on his birthday, and we can share it with him.'

It wasn't very nice for Lenny. He didn't have any cards to show the class, and he couldn't think of a birthday present to tell us about. He couldn't even think of

anything funny to say out of the corner of his mouth. He just had to stand there looking foolish until Miss Blake started the singing of 'Happy Birthday' – and then half the people didn't bother to sing it. I felt very sorry for him, I can tell you. But that wasn't the worst. The worst happened in the playground. I went to take his head end for bumps, and no one would come and take his feet. They all walked away. I had to finish up just patting him on the head with my hands, and before I knew what was coming out I was telling him, 'You can come home to tea with me, for your birthday.' And he said, yes, he would come.

My father works very hard in the Post Office, in a corner of our shop; and my mother stands at the door all day, where people pay for their groceries. When I get home from school, I carry cardboard boxes out to the yard and jump on them, or my big sister Nalini shows me which shelves to fill and I fill them with jam or chapatis – or birthday cards. On this day, though, I thought I'd use my key and go in through the side door and take Lenny straight upstairs – then hurry down again and tell my mum and dad that I'd got a friend in for an hour. I thought, I can get a birthday card and some cake and ice-cream from the shop, and Lenny can go home before they come upstairs. I wanted him to do that before my dad saw who it was, because he knows Lenny from his hanging around the shops.

Lenny said some funny things on the way home from school, but you know, I couldn't relax and enjoy them properly. I felt ashamed because I was wishing all the time that I hadn't asked him to come home with me. The bottoms of his trousers dragged along the ground, he had no buttons on his shirt so the sleeves flapped, and his hair must have made it hard for him to see where he was going.

I was in luck because the shop was very busy. My dad had a queue of people to pay out, and my mum had a crowd at the till. I left Lenny in the living-room and I went down to get what I wanted from the shop. I found him a birthday card with a badge in it. When I came back, he was sitting in a chair and the television was switched on. He's a good one at helping himself, I thought. We watched some cartoons and then we played 'Monopoly', which Lenny had seen on the shelf. We had some crisps and cakes and lemonade while we were playing; but I had only one eye on my 'Monopoly' moves – the other eye was on the clock all the time. I was getting very impatient for the game to finish, because it looked as if Lenny would still be there when they came up from the shop. I did some really bad moves so

that I could lose quickly, but it's very difficult to hurry up 'Monopoly', as you may know.

In the end I did such stupid things - like buying too many houses and selling Park Lane and Mayfair - that he won the game. He must have noticed what I was

doing, but he didn't say anything to me. Hurriedly, I gave him his birthday card. He pretended not to take very much notice of it, but he put it in his shirt, and kept feeling it to make sure it was still there. At least, that's what I thought he was making sure about, there inside his shirt.

It was just the right time to say goodbye, and I'm just thinking he can go without anyone seeing him, when my sister came in. She had run up from the shop for something or other, and she put her head inside the room. At some other time, I would have laughed out loud at her stupid face. When she saw Lenny, she looked as if she'd opened the door and seen something really unpleasant. I could gladly have given her a good kick. She shut the door a lot quicker than she opened it, and I felt really bad about it.

'Nice to meet you,' Lenny joked, but his face said he wanted to go, too, and I wasn't going to be the one to stop him.

I let him out, and I heaved a big sigh. I felt good about being kind to him, the way you do when you've done a sponsored swim, and I'd done it without my mum and dad frowning at me about who I brought home. Only Nalini had seen him, and everyone knows she can make things seem worse than they are. I washed the glasses, and I can remember singing while I stood at the sink. I was feeling very pleased with myself.

My good feeling lasted about fifteen minutes; just long enough to be wearing off slightly. Then Nalini came in again and destroyed it altogether.

'Prakash, have you seen that envelope that was on the television top?' she asked. 'I put it on here when I came in from school.'

'No,' I said. It was very soon to be getting worried, but things inside me were turning over like clothes in a washing-machine. I knew already where all this was going to end up. 'What was in it?' My voice sounded to me as if it was coming from a great distance.

She was looking everywhere in the room, but she kept coming back to the television top as if the envelope would mysteriously appear there. She stood there now, staring at me. '*What was in it?* What was in it was only a Postal Order for five pounds! Money for my school trip!'

'What does it look like?' I asked, but I think we both knew that I was only stalling. We both knew where it had gone.

'It's a white piece of paper in a brown envelope. It says "Postal Order" on it, in red.'

My washing-machine inside nearly went into a fast spin when I heard that. It was certainly Lenny's Red-Letter Day! But how could he be so ungrateful, I thought, when I was the only one to be kind to him? I clenched my fist while I pretended to look around. I wanted to punch him hard on the nose.

Then Nalini said what was in both our minds. 'It's that dirty kid who's got it. I'm going down to tell Dad. I don't know what makes you so stupid.'

Right at that moment I didn't know what made me so stupid, either, as to leave him up there on his own. I should have known. Didn't Miss Banks once say something about leopards never changing their spots?

When the shop closed, there was an awful business in the room. My dad was shouting-angry at me, and my mum couldn't think of anything good to say.

'You know where this boy lives,' my dad said. 'Tell me now, while I telephone the police. There's only one way of dealing with this sort of thing. If I go up there, I shall only get a mouthful of abuse. As if it isn't bad

enough for you to see me losing things out of the shop, you have to bring untrustworthy people upstairs!'

My mum saw how unhappy I was, and she tried to make things better. 'Can't you cancel the Postal Order?' she asked him.

'Of course not. Even if he hasn't had the time to cash it somewhere else by now, how long do you think the Post Office would let me be Sub-Postmaster if I did that sort of thing?'

I was feeling very bad for all of us, but the thought of the police calling at Lenny's house was making me feel worse.

'I'll get it back,' I said. 'I'll go to his house. It's only along the road from the school. And if I don't get it back, I can get the exact number of where he lives. *Then* you can telephone the police.' I had never spoken to my dad like that before, but I was feeling all shaky inside, and all the world seemed a different place to me that evening. I didn't give anybody a chance to argue with me. I ran straight out of the room and down to the street.

My secret hopes of seeing Lenny before I got to his house didn't come to anything. All too quickly I was there, pushing back his broken gate and walking up the cracked path to his front door. There wasn't a door knocker. I flapped the letter-box, and I started to think my dad was right. The police would have been better doing this than me.

I had never seen his mother before, only heard about her from other kids who lived near. When she opened the door, I could see she was a small lady with a tight mouth and eyes that said, 'Who are you?' and 'Go away from here!' at the same time.

She opened the door only a little bit, ready to slam it on me. I had to be quick.

'Is Lenny in, please?' I asked her.

She said, 'What's it to you?'

'He's a friend of mine,' I told her. 'Can I see him, please?'

She made a face as if she had something nasty in her mouth. 'LENNY!' she shouted. 'COME HERE!'

Lenny came slinking down the passage, like one of those scared animals in a circus. He kept his eyes on her hands, once he'd seen who it was at the door. There weren't any funny remarks coming from him.

She jerked her head at me. 'How many times have I told you not to bring kids to the house?' she shouted at him. She made it sound as if she was accusing him of a bad crime.

Lenny had nothing to say. She was hanging over him like a vulture about to fix its talons into a rabbit. It

looked so out of place that it didn't seem real. Then it came to me that it could be play-acting – the two of them. He had given her the five pounds, and she was putting this on to get rid of me quickly.

But suddenly she slammed the door so hard in my face I could see how the glass in it came to be broken.

'Well, I don't want kids coming to my door!' she shouted at him on the other side. 'Breaking the gate, breaking the windows, wearing out the path. How can I keep this place nice when I'm forever dragging to the door?'

She hit him then, I know she did. There was no play-acting about the bang as a foot hit the door, and Lenny yelling out loud as if a desk lid had come down on his head. But I didn't stop to hear any more. I'd heard enough to turn my stomach sick. Poor Lenny – I'd been worried about my mum and dad seeing him – and look what happened when his mother saw me! She had to be mad, that woman. And Lenny had to live with her! I didn't feel like crying, although my eyes had a hot rawness in them. More than anything, I just wanted to be back at home with my own family and the door shut tight.

Seeing my dad's car turn the corner was as if my dearest wish had been granted. He was going slowly, searching for me, with Nalini sitting up in front with big eyes. I waved, and ran to them. I got in the back and I drew in my breath to tell them to go straight home. It was worth fifty pounds not to have them knocking at Lenny's house, never mind five. But they were too busy trying to speak to me.

'Have you been to the house? Did you say anything?'

'Yes, I've been to the house, but –'

'Did you accuse him?'

'No. I didn't have a chance –'

They both sat back in their seats, as if the car would drive itself home.

'Well, we must be grateful for that.'

'We found the Postal Order.'

I could hardly believe what my ears were hearing. *They had found the Postal Order.* Lenny hadn't taken it, after all!

'It wasn't in its envelope,' Nalini was saying. 'He must have taken it out of that when he was tempted by it. But we can't accuse him of screwing up an envelope and hiding it in his pocket.'

'No, no,' I was saying, urging her to get on with things and tell me. 'So where was it?'

'In with the "Monopoly" money. He couldn't put it back on the television, so he must have kept it in his pile of "Monopoly" money, and put it back in the box.'

'Oh.'

'Mum found it. In all the commotion after you went out she knocked the box off the chair, and when she picked the bits up, there was the Postal Order.'

'It's certainly a good job you said nothing about it,' my dad said. 'And a good job I didn't telephone the police. We should have looked very small.'

All I could think was how small I had just felt, standing at Lenny's slammed door and hearing what his mother had said to him. And what about him getting beaten for having a friend call at his house?

My dad tried to be cheerful. 'Anyway, who won?' he asked.

'Lenny won the "Monopoly",' I said.

In bed that night, I lay awake a long time, thinking about it all. Lenny had taken some hard punishment from his mother. Some Red-Letter Day it had turned out to be! He would bear some hard thoughts about Prakash Patel.

He didn't come to school for a long time after that. But when he did, my heart sank into my boots. He came straight across the playground, the same flappy sleeves and dragging trouser bottoms, the same long, tangled hair – and he came straight for me. What would he do? Hit me? Spit in my face?

As he got close, I saw what was on his shirt, pinned there like a medal. It was his birthday badge.

'It's a good game, that "Monopoly",' he said out of the corner of his mouth. It was as if he was trying to tell me something.

'Yes,' I said. 'It's a good game all right.'

I hadn't got the guts to tell him that I'd gone straight home that night and thrown it in the dustbin. Dealings with houses didn't appeal to me any more.

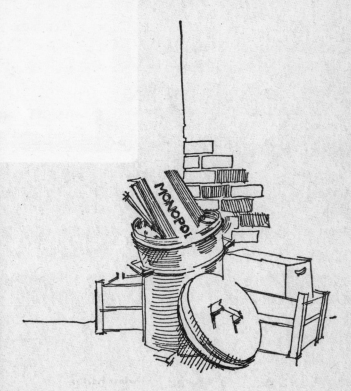